Best Sincere
Wishes.
Pat Stodghill
Poet Laureate of Texas

Rita
Read to your
Grandchildren —

from
Tommie

(Pat is my sister)

Jake's snapping Catastrophe

Written by
Pat Stodghill

Illustrated by
Rita Briley

EAKIN PRESS ◆ Austin, Texas

FIRST EDITION

Copyright © 2000
By Pat Stodghill
Illustrated by Rita Briley

Published in the United States of America
By Eakin Press
A Division of Sunbelt Media, Inc.
P.O. Box 90159
Austin, TX 78709
email: eakinpub@sig.net

1 2 3 4 5 6 7 8 9

1-57168-379-8

For CIP information, please access:
www.loc.gov

For Jake, my grandson

*Thanks to Sandy Grubb, SAGE teacher, for her encouragement and to
Sheri Stodghill Fowler, my daughter, for her work on this book.*

Jacob Hall Fowler
Rode in his wagon.
He played with each toy,
And everyone said,
"He's a very good boy!"

He loved his handsome dad, Kevin,
And his pretty mom, Sheri Sue,
But there were times when it seemed
He had nothing to do.

He watched Sesame Street and circuses
On his TV set,
But something seemed missing;
He sighed with regret,
That there were so many animals
In the world, and yet,
Jacob Hall Fowler had only
Two dogs to pet.

Gatsby was a dachshund
And Ginger was a dane.
Jake would bark like a dog,
And act crazy, insane.
He would crawl on the floor.
He would laugh and would shout.
Then all three would run in a circle
Until their tongues would hang out.

Jake's mom had decorated
His room like a zoo,
With a big Noah's Ark
And all the animals too.

Jake growled at the tigers,
To the ducks said, "Quack! Quack!"
He roared at the lions,
Said "Meow" to the cats,
But not one single animal
Even spoke back.

He scurried like a squirrel,
Hopped like a kangaroo.
He said, "Come down from the wall
And I'll play games with you."

Not an animal moved.
Not one blinked an eye.
Not one bird stirred a feather.
Jake wanted to cry.

Then he held his stuffed monkey.
He hugged Bruce, his bear.
He reached for Charlie elephant,
But all they did was stare.

So Jake called and he called,
"Mommy! Mommy! It's no fun at all
To pet giraffes or parakeets
That are just painted on the wall,
Or stuffed animals who smile or frown,
But won't play with me at all!"

Sheri Sue looked at the ceiling.
She looked at the floor.
She looked at the walls,
And she looked at the door.

Finally, she said, "Jake,
I haven't a clue,
But we will call your grandma.
She'll know what to do."

So Grandma came over
As fast as a wink,
Or at least as fast as it would take
A submarine to sink.

She hugged Jake and said,
"You must have some magic without delay.
We will visit my friend, Mr. Bradbury Ray.
He has answers before you ask questions,
They say.

"His hair is as white as silver,
His eyes bright as stars;
And he knows everything
About Jupiter, Venus, or Mars.

"He is the wisest of wizards,
But he is a caring man, too.
I'll bet a bag of peanuts
He will have an answer for you."

When they arrived,
Mr. Ray looked right at Jake
And said, "I can see
Amazing things will happen to you
If you learn to let
The magic come through.

"But you must wish
Only for good things
If you want the power
That this magic brings.

"Is he a good boy?"
Asked Mr. Bradbury Ray.
Grandma said, "A very good boy.
In fact, he is A++ O.K."

"Then repeat after me,"
Said Mr. Bradbury Ray,
"I will care. I will share.
I will do what is right
With all of my might.

"Then close your eyes,
Make a wish,
And snap your fingers
With a twist of your wrist."

Jake repeated the words.
Then his eyes opened wide.
"I don't know how to snap my fingers
And I really, really tried."

"You will learn. It takes time,"
Said Mr. Bradbury Ray.
"There are mountains to climb.
There are doors to walk through.
If you just look around,
You will find plenty to do."

Grandma said, "Thank you," and smiled
As she drove away.
Then she said to Jake, "You need a nap,
Young man, after such a big day."

So Jake would say the special words
Each time before his nap,
But he just couldn't get
His fingers to snap.
He thought and he thought:
"There must be some trick . . .
Some mystical magic
To get fingers to click!"

Time passed . . . . . . And then

One night at a quarter to four
Kevin and Sheri heard a squeak,
And a growl, and a terrible roar.
They rushed fast as lightning
To Jake's bedroom door.

"Mommy and Daddy,
Look what has happened.
My dream has come true,"
Said Jake smiling proudly,
"I've invented a zoo!

"But I only wished for one
Instead of a pair
And only baby animals,
And none that would scare."
"Thank goodness!" said Sheri
As she collapsed in a chair.

"A baby whale would be too big for our bathtub.
A baby elephant might fall through our floor.
There are no lizards or snakes,
No centipedes or dragons,
Not even one dinosaur!

"An octopus could make a mess,
Grabbing things with all eight arms,
So I tried not to wish for anything
That would cause anybody harm."

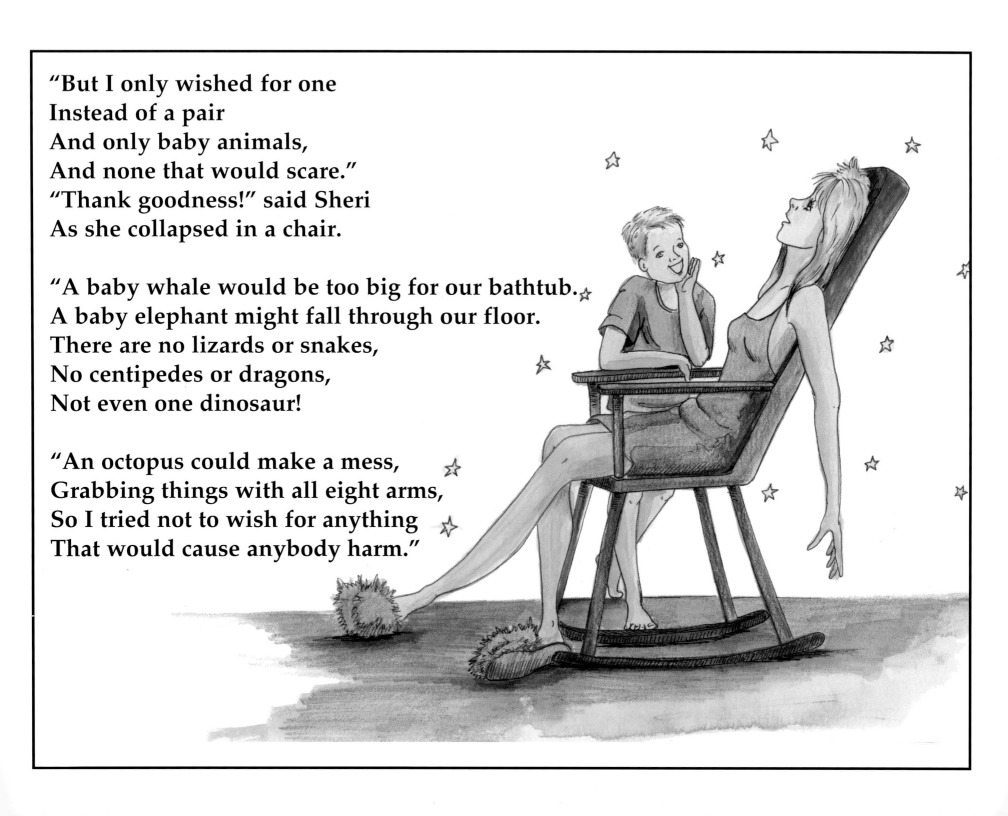

"Thank you, Jake," said his mom
From her rocking chair,
As a rabbit cuddled in her lap;
A hummingbird perched in her hair.

Jake was so happy
He stood straight up in his bed.
He hugged a baby giraffe's neck
And petted a sheep's shaggy head.

"Oh, goodness! Oh, gracious!
Oh, what shall we do?
We have a real problem," said Sheri,
"Because real animals love to chew."

The kitten clawed at the lace curtain
Beside the front door.
The deer ate an ivy plant,
Then started for more.

A baby goat went to the trash and grabbed a tin can,
And a monkey clung to the ceiling fan.
"Oh Kevin, get a banana," begged Sheri,
"Please make him come down."

A black-spotted calf with a brown face
said, "Moo!"
While a baby duck nibbled
On Jake's new tennis shoe.

A swan swam in the kitchen sink,
Not bothered at all
By the tall, shaggy camel
Who took a big drink.

A chipmunk chewed
On the pink and white couch.
Then he bit Kevin's leg,
And Kevin yelled, "Ouch!"

A pig squealed
As he ran through the house,
Knocked over a table,
And almost stepped on a mouse.

The animals scampered and scurried.
They slipped and they slid.
They climbed, kicked, and cuddled.
They huddled and hid.

Sheri said, "This must stop!
This must stop . . . This very minute.
They are ruining our house,
And we must live in it."

So Sheri and Kevin agreed:
"ALL ANIMALS MUST GO!"
But Jake started crying,
"Oh, no! No! No! No!"

As a little cub started chewing
The rug on the floor,
Grandma came into the house . . .
Right through the front door.

"Don't fret and don't frown
I know what we will do.
Our town is in great need
Of a new petting zoo."

So she went to the phone
And called up the chief,
While Sheri and Kevin
Breathed sighs of relief.

In exchange for these wonderful animals,
The town will clean and repair
All the damage and havoc
They have caused here and there.

But Jake wasn't smiling.
Tears rolled down his cheeks.
"I'll never see my friends again.
We won't even get to speak."

"Oh Jake," said Grandma,
"This isn't the end.
Now every week we can go to the zoo;
You can visit your friends.
But you must promise me;
You won't make this wish again."

So Jake hugged each animal
And with a smile on his face,
Told them how special they were
To get to go to this special place.

"Lots of kids, not just me,
Will get to meet you.
So I'll be seeing you soon
At the new petting zoo!"